Where Have You Been, Little Cat?

For Moppet

SIMON & SCHUSTER

First published in Great Britain in 2022 by Simon & Schuster
UK Ltd, 1st Floor, 222 Gray's Inn Road, London WC1X 8HB

Text and illustrations copyright © 2022 Richard Jones

A CIP catalogue record for this book is available from
the British Library upon request

ISBN: 978-1-3985-0252-9 (HB)
ISBN: 978-1-3985-0253-6 (eBook)

Printed in China
1 3 5 7 9 10 8 6 4 2

Where Have You Been, Little Cat?

Richard Jones

SIMON & SCHUSTER

London New York Sydney Toronto New Delhi

We have a little cat.

When she wants to come in,
she taps on the front door.

She rushes past me, so happy to be home again.

She curls her tail around my legs
and I tickle her under her chin.

I always ask her, "Where have you been, little cat?

Where did you go?

Who did you meet?

What did you see?

What did you hear?

Were you happy?

Were you scared?

Were you brave?

Were you kind?

What did you do?

Where *did* you go?"

She presses her soft head against mine. And I always say to her, "I'm glad you're home, little cat."